Dora Loves Her Family

Written by Christine Ricci

Illustrated by A&J Studios, Dave Aikins, Tom Mangano, Zina Saunders, and Steve Savitsky

Louis Weber, C.E.O.
Publications International, Ltd.
7373 North Cicero Avenue, Lincolnwood, Illinois 60712
Ground Floor, 59 Gloucester Place, London W1U 8JJ

Customer Service: 1-800-595-8484 or customer_service@pilbooks.com

www.pilbooks.com

Permission is never granted for commercial purposes.

Manufactured in China.

p i kids is a registered trademark of Publications International, Ltd.

8 7 6 5 4 3 2 1

ISBN-13: 978-1-4127-8924-0
ISBN-10: 1-4127-8924-9

publications international, ltd.

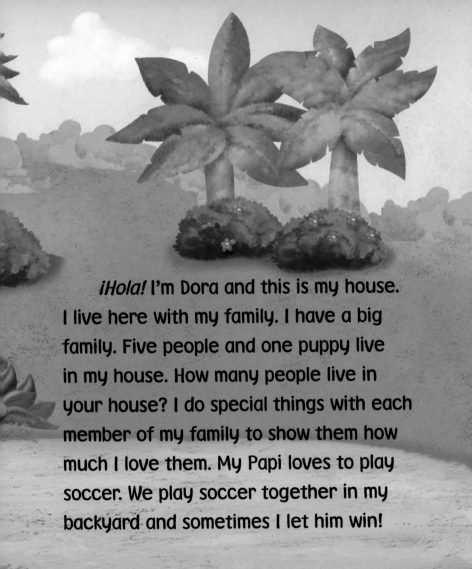

¡Hola! I'm Dora and this is my house. I live here with my family. I have a big family. Five people and one puppy live in my house. How many people live in your house? I do special things with each member of my family to show them how much I love them. My Papi loves to play soccer. We play soccer together in my backyard and sometimes I let him win!

My Mami and I love to explore together. She's an archaeologist! That's a kind of explorer. I help her dig for ancient treasure! We find beautiful rocks, vases, coins, and all kinds of jewels. Maybe when I grow up, I'll be an archaeologist just like her!

I'm a big sister! The babies like it when I play with them. I roll the ball to them and they roll it back to me! They giggle when we play peekaboo! Every night, I tell them a bedtime story. The babies love to hear adventure stories! I love spending time with my baby brother and sister!

I like to visit my Abuela. Sometimes I even stay overnight!

We bake our favorite treats and she tells me stories about Explorer Stars! Did you know that my Abuela was a Star Catcher just like me? She gave me my Star Pocket! I really like spending time with my Abuela!

My puppy Perrito is part of my family, too. I give him lots of hugs and kisses so he knows how much I love him. And I make sure that he has food and water and lots of exercise so he stays healthy.

Sometimes, just taking care
of someone shows them that you
love them!

We have a family dinner at my house every night. We laugh and tell stories while we eat together. Each of us gets a turn to tell everyone about our day. What do you talk about at your family dinners?

My family likes to spend holidays
together! We go to each others' houses
for parties!

I like celebrating holidays with my whole family. I especially like visiting my cousin, Diego. Who do you like to visit?

I love spending time with everyone in my family. Sometimes the best way for me to make sure that my family knows that I love them is just to tell them! I say "I love you" to everyone in my family! Who do you say "I love you" to?